Dora and Diego to the Rescue!

W9-AAN-627

Based on the TV series *Go, Diego, Go*™ as seen on Nick Jr.™

Simon Spotlight/Nickelodeon
An imprint of Simon & Schuster Children's Publishing Division
New York   Chicago   Toronto   Sydney
1230 Avenue of the Americas, New York, NY 10020

Manufactured in the United States of America 0113 LAK
This Simon Spotlight edition 2010
4 6 8 10 9 7 5 3
ISBN 978-1-4424-0660-5
These titles were previously published individually by Simon Spotlight.

DIEGO'S GREAT DINOSAUR RESCUE

adapted by Sheila Sweeny Higginson
based on the original teleplay written by Valerie Walsh
illustrated by Art Mawhinney

"*¡Hola!*" said Diego. "I'm Diego, and I came to the dinosaur museum to study some animals that lived long ago. Do you see who came with me? Baby Jaguar, my sister Alicia, and even *mi prima*, Dora."

"*¡Hola!*" said Alicia. "Do you want to learn about dinosaurs with us?"

"*¡Vámonos!*" said Dora. "Let's go see the museum!"

Alicia looked around at the many dinosaur skeletons in the museum. "Dinosaurs came in all different shapes and sizes," she said.

"Diego, do you see a superbig dinosaur with a really long neck?" Alicia asked.

"*¡Sí!* There it is!" said Diego. "The Brachiosaurus."

"And I see a really small dinosaur," said Dora. "Do you?"

"There!" said Alicia. "The Microraptor! It's so small that it could fit in Backpack!"

Baby Jaguar rushed over to a dinosaur skeleton that was surrounded by eggs. "Alicia, what kind of dinosaur is this one?" he asked.

"That one is called a Maiasaura," Alicia answered.

"What do you think happened to it?" Diego asked.

Alicia walked over to a book near the Maiasaura. As she turned the pages, she began to tell a story about the dinosaur.

"Once upon a time," Alicia began, "there was a very brave dinosaur named Maia. Maia was the big sister in a Maiasaura family. The Maiasaura family traveled together, looking for a place to lay their dinosaur eggs. But one day while they were walking, Maia sniffed the air and looked worried."

"Why?" Baby Jaguar asked.

"Maia smelled Troodon dinosaurs," Alicia said. "Maiasauras are afraid of Troodons."

"What happened next, Alicia?" Dora asked.

"Maia told her brothers and sisters to catch up to their *mami* while she stayed behind to build a wall that the Troodons could not get over."

"Smart thinking!" said Diego.

"Maia worked hard to protect her family," Alicia continued, "but when she was finished, a storm came. It rained so hard that it washed away the footprints of Maia's family."

"Oh, no!" Diego cried. "Maia got lost!"

"We've got to help Maia the Maiasaura find her family!" said Diego. "It's our biggest adventure ever, but I know we can do it because I'm an Animal Rescuer!"

"I'm an Animal Scientist," added Alicia. "I know a lot about dinosaurs!"

"I'm an explorer!" said Dora. "I've traveled all over the world!"

"Don't forget about me!" said Baby Jaguar. "I am a jaguar, and I can growl really loud!"

"We need to jump back to the time of the dinosaurs," Diego said.

"Are you ready to jump back 120 million years?" asked Alicia.

"*¡Salta!*" said Dora as she jumped.

Diego, Dora, Alicia, and Baby Jaguar sailed through the air and landed in a place filled with giant trees and swampy ponds.

"We made it! Now we can help Maia get back to her family," said Diego. "But I don't see her anywhere."

"Look!" called Dora. "There are dinosaur footprints on the ground."

Baby Jaguar looked puzzled. "But we don't know which ones are Maia's footprints."

"My book says that Maiasauras have three toes. So we just need to look for the footprints with three toes."

Diego counted the toes on each footprint. Finally he pointed to one and said, "*¡Uno, dos, tres!* Three toes! That must be Maia's footprint! *¡Al rescate!* To the rescue!"

"Look, Diego," called Alicia. "There's Maia the Maiasaura!"

Diego ran down the path toward the dinosaur. "*¡Hola, Maia!*" Diego called, but Maia could not hear him.

"I've got an idea!" Baby Jaguar said as he jumped up and down. "If we roar really loud like a dinosaur, Maia will hear us."

"Great idea, Baby Jaguar!" Diego said. "Everyone roar to call Maia."

Maia heard the roars and leaned down to Diego.

"We've come to help you find your family," Diego told Maia.

"*¡Gracias, amigos!*" Maia said thankfully.

"Map can help us find your family," said Dora as she held out Map.

Map showed them the path to Maia's family. "Maia's family is on Egg Island," said Map. "To get to Egg Island, first you go through the Muddy Mud Pits. Then you go across the Rocky Rock Cliffs and past the Volcano. And that's how you'll get to Egg Island!"

"*¡Vámonos!* Let's go!" cheered Dora.

"We made it to the Muddy Mud Pits!" Dora shouted.

Suddenly they heard a rumbling noise. "That's my tummy growling because I'm hungry," Maia said.

"We'll find you something to eat," Diego said.

"Some dinosaurs were meat eaters," Alicia said. "Other dinosaurs were plant eaters."

"What does Maia like to eat?" asked Diego.

"Lots and lots of leaves!" boomed Maia.

"So we need to find some trees with leaves!" said Alicia. "Do you see any?"

At the trees Maia stood on her back legs and stretched up to eat the yummy leaves.

"Let's all stretch like a Maiasaura!" Diego yelled. "Stretch, stretch, stretch!"

After the snack the friends made their way to the Rocky Rock Cliffs.

"Look out!" Diego warned. "There's a rock slide!" The ground shook, and suddenly Diego, Alicia, and Dora were carried down the cliff by a pile of rocks.

"Diego," said Dora, as she pointed to the top of the cliff, "we've got to get back to the top so we can take Maia to her family."

"What can we use to climb up the rock cliff?" Diego asked.

"You can use my tail!" Maia cheered.

On the way to Egg Island, Maia smelled Troodons again.

"Oh, no!" Diego said worriedly. "Maiasauras are afraid of Troodons!"

"'Troodons are really smart dinosaurs,'" Alicia read from her dinosaur book.

"They're not as smart as us," Diego said. "If we all stomp like big dinosaurs, they'll think there's an earthquake and we'll scare them away."

"Quick!" said Dora. "Let's all stand up and stomp like dinosaurs!"

Diego's plan worked! The Troodons were tricked and they ran far, far away. Baby Jaguar looked across the water at Egg Island. "How will we get to the island?" he asked.

"I can swim!" Maia said to Baby Jaguar.

"That's right!" said Alicia. "Maiasauras and a lot of other dinosaurs can swim."

Finally Maia reached Egg Island and was reunited with her family. Her *mami* and *papi* were so happy to see her.

"Thank you for helping Maia find her way back to us," said Mommy Maiasaura.

"You're welcome," answered Diego. "*¡Misión cumplida!* Rescue complete!"

"We learned a lot while visiting the time of the dinosaurs, but now it's time to head back to the museum," Alicia said.

"*¡Vámonos!*" shouted Dora. And with that, Diego, Baby Jaguar, Alicia, and Dora jumped back to the museum to continue their dinosaur adventures another day.

Did you know?

GOOD MOM

Maiasaura means "Good Mother Lizard."

SMALL AND SPEEDY

Troodons were small and speedy. They were also smart—they had very large brains for dinosaurs.

WING IT

Microraptors had winged arms and legs.

BIG BOY

A Brachiosaurus was about as long as two school buses and as tall as a four-story building.

THEY'RE EVERYWHERE!

Dinosaurs lived on all of the continents.

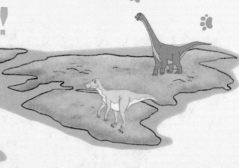

Diego's Wolf Pup Rescue

adapted by Christine Ricci

based on the original teleplay written by Valerie Walsh

illustrated by Art Mawhinney

"We're Animal Rescuers!" shouted Diego as he slid down the pole from the Animal Rescue Center's observation platform.

"Animal Rescuers!" chanted his cousin Dora as she followed Diego down the pole.

Dora was visiting the Animal Rescue Center, and Diego had a special surprise for her.

"Watch this!" said Diego as he cupped his hand to his mouth and called, "Ah-ruff! Ah-ruff!"

Suddenly several maned wolf pups poked their heads out of the tall grass. *"Ah-ruff! Ah-ruff!"* they barked.

"Maned wolf pups!" said Dora excitedly. "What a great surprise!"

The pups playfully scampered over to Diego and Dora.
"They're so small!" giggled Dora as the pups climbed on her.
"And this one is the littlest," said Diego as he stroked the tiny pup's fur.

Just then Diego's sister Alicia arrived with Mommy Maned Wolf. "Mommy Maned Wolf came to the Rescue Center to have her wolf pups," Alicia explained.

Dora turned to Mommy Maned Wolf. "Your little pups are so cute. And there are so many of them!"

"Maned wolves can have up to five pups at a time," Mommy Maned Wolf said proudly.

"How many pups are there?" asked Diego. "Let's count them."

Dora and Diego counted the wolf pups: one, two, three, four. Four maned wolf pups!

Mommy Maned Wolf gasped. "Only *four* maned wolf pups?" she asked. "But I have *five* pups! My littlest pup is missing!"

"Don't worry, Mommy Maned Wolf!" said Diego. "We're Animal Rescuers. We'll find your littlest pup."

Alicia decided to stay at the Animal Rescue Center to help Mommy Maned Wolf with the other pups. "Go, Animal Rescuers! Go!" she cheered as Diego and Dora ran off toward the Science Deck.

Diego and Dora ran over to their special camera, Click.
"Click can help us find the baby maned wolf," said Diego.

Click zoomed through the forest and found the little wolf pup.

"He's heading for the prickers and thorns!" said Diego, watching closely. "He could get hurt."

"We've got to rescue him!" said Dora.

"*¡Al rescate!*" shouted Diego. "To the rescue!"

Diego and Dora jumped on a zip cord and zoomed through the forest. They landed at a fork in the road. "Look!" said Diego. "There are prints on each path."

"But which ones belong to the baby maned wolf?" Dora asked.

Diego pulled out his Field Journal and scrolled to a picture of a maned wolf's paw print. "Which path has prints that look like these?" he asked.

"These prints match," exclaimed Dora as she pointed to the third path. "*¡Vámonos!* Let's go!"

The path led them to a river. Diego pulled out his spotting scope and located the wolf pup's prints on the far bank. "We need to get across this river to keep following the wolf pup's tracks," said Diego.

"I can help!" called out Rescue Pack.

"Me too!" chimed in Backpack.

Rescue Pack and Backpack worked together to help get Diego and Dora across the river. Rescue Pack transformed himself into a raft. Backpack gave them paddles and a life jacket.

After turning his vest into a second life jacket, Diego jumped into the raft next to Dora. They started to paddle down the river. Suddenly Diego noticed a river otter stuck in a whirlpool. "We have to rescue the river otter!" he shouted.

Diego threw a life preserver to the river otter, and the river otter scrambled onto it. Then Diego and Dora pulled the river otter to safety.

"Thanks for rescuing me," said the river otter.

"We're Animal Rescuers," replied Diego. "It's what we do!"

Once on shore Diego and Dora ran toward the prickers and thorns. But when they arrived, the little maned wolf was nowhere in sight. Diego cupped his hands to his ears to listen for the pup. Finally he heard a bark.

"Ah-ruff!"

"It sounds like he's in these bushes," said Diego.

Diego and Dora stretched up tall to see over the pricker and thorn bushes.

The little maned wolf was heading toward a sharp prickly bush!
"Stop, Baby Maned Wolf!" called Diego and Dora. "Stop!"
Baby Maned Wolf heard the warning and stopped right in front of the
sharp prickly bush.

Diego and Dora ran over to the little wolf pup and knelt down next to him.

"Hi, Baby Maned Wolf!" Diego said. "We're Animal Rescuers! You're safe now!"

"Thanks for rescuing me," said Baby Maned Wolf. "I can't wait to see my Mommy and my brothers and sisters."

Back at the Animal Rescue Center, Mommy Maned Wolf nuzzled her littlest pup and made sure he wasn't hurt. Baby Maned Wolf was so happy to be with his family that he jumped into Diego's arms and gave him a big lick on the cheek.

Then Baby Maned Wolf curled up next to the other pups and fell fast asleep.

"*¡Misión cumplida!* Rescue complete!" whispered Diego. "That was a great animal adventure!"

Did you know?

The MANE event!

The maned wolf is called maned because it grows a mane of long black hair on its back.

A leg up!

Maned wolves live in grasslands and swampy areas. The maned wolf's long legs allow it to see over tall grass.

Howl are you?

Maned wolves talk to each other by howling.

My, what big ears you have!

Maned wolves can rotate their large ears to listen for other animals. They have excellent hearing!